THE ALPHA TRACKER

A STEAMY PROTECTIVE ALPHA OMEGAVERSE ROMANCE

ASH JADE

Dear Reader,

Welcome to *Rescued by the Rider.*

This is an omegaverse romance—a version of the world where people have secondary dynamics (alpha, beta, omega) that affect scent, pheromones, and instinct. In this story, those instincts can be loud, but they don't get to make decisions for anyone. What matters here is choice: communication, consent, and the steady, hard-earned work of building trust.

A few things to know before you begin:

This book includes material that may be difficult for some readers. I keep a detailed, up-to-date list of content warnings on my website (so you can check what you need without spoilers):

https://www.ashjadeauthor.com/pages/content
-warnings

Intimate scenes are explicit and consent-centered. Every touch is asked for, every boundary honored. And while the road is steep, this is still a romance with a guaranteed HEA.

If you're ready for a protective alpha who earns it, an omega who refuses to be owned, and a love built on choice instead of instinct, turn the page.

— Ash Jade

Contents

1

CALLAN

The call comes while I'm cleaning blood from under my fingernails. Sheriff Rawlins doesn't waste time with pleasantries, just grunts my name like a question mark and tells me he's got a missing omega that needs finding. Fast. I scrub harder at the dried flecks—remnants of the buck I'd field-dressed this morning—but they cling like they belong there.

"When?" I ask, wedging the phone between shoulder and ear.

"Three weeks ago. Trafficking operation. She escaped before they could get her to auction."

My jaw tightens. Trafficking. "Any trail?"

"Cold by now, but there've been sightings. Wilderness area, northeast sector." Jake pauses. "This one's different, Hodge. She knows how to hide."

I grunt acknowledgment, already mentally packing, calculating distances, weather patterns. "I'll be there in an hour."

The sheriff's office smells like bad coffee. Jake looks older than the last time I saw him—new creases around his eyes, a certain heaviness to his shoulders that comes from carrying too much of other people's trouble.

"Sienna Bishop," he says, sliding a thin file across his desk. "Twenty-four. Taken from a bus station in Portland. Transport vehicle crashed near the ridge—looks like she used the opportunity."

I flip through the sparse information. The photo shows a woman with wary eyes and a stubborn set to her jaw. She doesn't look scared. She looks ready for a fight.

"They've sent others?" I ask. Traffickers don't let valuable merchandise walk away.

Jake nods.

"Two search teams we know of. Haven't returned." His mouth quirks, almost proud. "Like I said. She's smart."

I study the map where he's marked the last confirmed sightings. A pattern—moving steadily northeast, sticking to the roughest terrain. Choices a panicked omega wouldn't make.

"Anything else I should know?" I ask, folding the map into my pocket.

Jake's eyes flick to his office door, then back to me. He lowers his voice. "There are places, farther north. Beyond my jurisdiction. They handle situations like this... differently."

"Different how?"

"Don't ask questions I can't officially answer, Hodge." He pushes an envelope across the desk. As he draws his hand back, his sleeve rides up—a braided leather cord around his wrist, threaded with a small iron charm. An antler. He catches me looking and tugs the cuff down without comment. "Your advance. Find her before they do."

I pack. Extra clothes, first aid supplies, enough food for ten days. Weapons—visible and concealed. Routine work—locate the target, make the extraction, collect the fee.

My truck growls up mountain roads as the first hint of dawn cracks the sky. I find her first known campsite near a stream bend. Kneeling, I brush my fingers over the ground. The imprint of a small body, but not curled in fear. Stretched out, watchful. I lift a handful of dirt, bring it to my nose. A faint trace of lemon—and the metallic tang of something else. Iron. The scent hooks somewhere low in my brain, and heat rolls through me—sudden, startling, wholly disproportionate to a trace three days cold. My fingers curl into the dirt. No human nose should catch a scent like this. But alpha senses aren't entirely human. Something older, coded into the marrow, a predator's inheritance that no biologist has fully explained. The scent sharpens my vision at the edges, colors brightening to a clarity that would alarm me if I weren't used to it—the hunt response, some call it. The thing in us that's more animal than man.

Five miles northeast, I find where she built a fire. Smart location—stone outcropping above, water nearby, multiple escape routes. The kind of spot only someone with training—or remarkable instinct—would choose. I circle the perimeter, piecing together her movements. Steady gait, chosen path—choices most people in her position wouldn't make.

This isn't someone running without a plan.

By midday, I've found three false trails. Each one starts convincingly—broken twigs, disturbed ground, even a hair tie placed to look accidental—then vanishes at precisely the point where a pursuer would be fully committed. I almost smile. She's not just surviving. She's hunting her hunters.

At her third campsite, I discover a small bundle of dried berries wrapped in a leaf. Stored on purpose. She's foraging systematically, preserving food, managing resources. The site itself shows careful camouflage—better than some military personnel I've tracked.

The sun dips low, shadows pooling across the forest floor, when I find them. Fresh tracks. Not more than six hours old. Small footprints with an unusual weight distribution—favoring the outer edge of the right foot. An old injury, maybe, or just adaptation to rough terrain.

I crouch, pressing my palm to the indentation. Still warm. She's alive. The relief is immediate—and so is the unease. Everything about this trail reads wrong for a frightened omega. Everything about Sienna Bishop defies what I was told to expect.

Standing, I scan the deepening shadows of the forest. Somewhere out there, she's moving. Watching, maybe. The skin at my nape tightens.

I'm being watched. And for the first time in a long time, I'm the one who feels outmatched.

I shoulder my pack, adjusting to the weight. Night's coming, and with it, the cold. I need shelter, need to process what I'm learning about my target. She's more than the file suggested. An omega who's survived everything thrown at her and is still fighting.

I push deeper into the darkening trees. But a decade of hunting tells me this much: Sienna Bishop might not want to be found at all.

2

SIENNA

He's good. Better than the others. I've been watching him for three days now, tracking the tracker, and he hasn't made a single amateur mistake. Moves like a ghost through the trees, reading signs most wouldn't see, disturbing nothing that doesn't need disturbing. An alpha, definitely—that much I can smell even from my perch twenty feet up this pine—but not like the others. He doesn't stomp or snap branches to mark territory—just quiet, patient hunting. The most dangerous kind.

I shift my weight slightly, careful not to rustle the branches. My muscles ache from holding still so long, but stillness keeps me alive. Below, he kneels beside the stream where I collected water yesterday, fingers testing the mud, nose lifting to catch traces of scent. His eyes narrow—sharp, assessing, missing nothing.

When he stands, I get a better look. Tall, broad-shouldered, but lean like someone who burns more calories than he consumes. Dark hair pulled back at the nape. Gun at his hip, knife at his ankle. Hunter's gear, practical, not the paramilitary crap the traffickers wear. My gaze catches on the exposed line of his throat, the way tendons shift when he turns his head. Something low in my belly tightens—not fear. I know fear. This is different, and I hate it immediately.

What makes my skin prickle isn't his weapons. It's how he treats my campsite.

He steps around the small circle of stones where I built my fire two nights ago. Doesn't kick them aside like the others did. Studies the arrangement, the half-burned sticks, but leaves them exactly as I positioned them. When he finds the tiny snare I rigged with shoelace and willow branch, he examines it without breaking the mechanism.

Almost like he respects the work.

My head throbs, and suddenly I'm not in the forest anymore.

The transport van jostles, throwing us against each other. Five omegas packed in darkness that reeks of fear and piss. Metal cuffs bite into my wrists. The woman next to me weeps silently, her tears dropping onto my shoulder.

"Shut the fuck up back there!" the driver shouts.

An older omega across from me catches my eye. Grey-streaked hair, face lined with hardship, but her gaze is steady, almost serene. Wrong for this place. She leans forward slightly, voice barely a whisper.

"Listen carefully, girl. If you get the chance, run north. Keep going north."

I stare. She must have been dreaming.

"There are riders," she continues, so softly I have to strain to hear over the engine. "Not the kind that sell or cage. The kind that make people disappear."

"Disappear where?" I breathe back.

Her eyes gleam in the darkness. "To safety. Real safety, not just another kind of cage. Places beyond the reach of alphas like these. Places where omegas choose." Her voice softens, almost reverent. "Cabins with doors that lock from the inside. Gardens behind stone walls. Children who've never been registered." She pauses, as if weighing how much to share. "A healer checks you over when you arrive—no restraints, no exam table. Just hands and herbs and someone who asks where it hurts."

The driver slams on the brakes, throwing us forward. The woman's head cracks against metal. She doesn't speak again.

I blink back to the present, to the pine sap sticky under my fingers and the alpha moving through my abandoned camp below. Fantasy. That's what

I'd thought at the time. Desperate fairy tales whispered by frightened omegas. No such places exist.

But then what did she mean by riders?

The alpha—tracker, whatever he is—moves with purpose toward the false trail I laid yesterday. I've set three branches to snap under a heavy footstep, rigged to sound like someone moving clumsily away from the stream. Most pursuers would leap at the obvious sign.

He doesn't.

Instead, he examines the ground, the pattern of disturbed leaves, and sits back on his haunches. His eyes scan the area with that same unhurried patience. Then he looks up, sweeping his gaze across the treetops.

I freeze, pressing against the trunk, though I know my hiding spot is good. Three days of watching has taught me his patterns. He'll search the high ground but won't climb unless he sees clear evidence. Still, my pulse kicks hard.

The sun slides toward the horizon. My stomach growls, a sharp reminder that I've stretched my supplies dangerously thin. Two protein bars left. Half a bag of nuts. Maybe enough for two more days if I forage. My muscles ache from constant movement, constant vigilance.

I need to decide.

He could be hired by the traffickers. Could be a bounty hunter. Could be law enforcement—though no cop I've ever met moves like that. If he's with them, revealing myself means returning to a cage, to the auction block, to whatever alpha paid the highest price.

If he's not with them... what? Another kind of cage, probably. Even "helpful" alphas expect something in return.

Places where omegas choose.

Fantasy. Has to be.

I watch him move toward my northeastern false trail. It's my best work—subtle enough to look unintentional, leading away from my actual path. I left a token there too, a small carved piece of wood I'd been working on to pass time at night. Not accidental. A test.

He follows the trail exactly as I expected, reading the signs, moving with that same quiet efficiency. When he finds the carving tucked beneath a rock, my breath catches.

He lifts it between thumb and forefinger. A small, crude wolf I shaped with my pocket knife. Not art—just something to keep my hands busy. He turns it over, examining the rough edges, the uneven lines.

What I don't expect is the way he handles it. No dismissive toss aside. No pocketing it as evidence. Instead, his thumb brushes across its surface almost... gently. Then he places it back exactly where I left it, arranging the rock to protect it from the elements.

Something shifts behind my ribs. I don't let myself name it.

He stands there a moment longer, eyes scanning the surrounding woods. For the briefest moment, his gaze passes over my hiding spot, and I could swear he pauses—but then he moves on, continuing along the false trail.

Only when he disappears from view do I allow myself to breathe normally again. Night will come soon. I need to move, find a new position, prepare more contingencies. My ankle throbs from three days in trees and rough terrain, but pain is just another sensation to manage.

I ease down from my perch, one limb at a time. Whatever this alpha wants, whoever sent him, I won't be easy prey. I've outmaneuvered six pursuers already. This one's better, but I'm desperate. And desperation makes for dangerous quarry.

Still, as I ghost through the darkening forest, those calloused fingers stay with me—the unexpected care in the way he handled my carving. A gentleness I haven't seen in longer than I can remember.

I set three new escape routes before finding a sheltered overhang for the night. As I chew slowly on half a protein bar, stretching the meager calories, I map tomorrow's strategy. Keep watching. Keep moving. Keep surviving.

And try not to think about riders who make people disappear into safety, or the way an alpha's hands can touch something breakable without breaking it. Or the heat that pooled low in my stomach watching him do it.

3

CALLAN

The bootprint appears where it shouldn't be—a heavy tread cutting across Sienna's more delicate trail. Not the first sign of interlopers I've found today, but the most concerning. These aren't random hikers or weekend warriors. The depth, the precision of placement, the effort to step exactly where she stepped—professional tracking. Military-grade. I crouch, fingers tracing the edge. Fresh. Less than six hours old. My skin prickles. I'm not alone in this hunt anymore.

I ghost through the underbrush, following the newcomers' trail rather than Sienna's. Better to know what I'm dealing with before making another move. The forest thickens as I ascend the ridge, offering better cover. Good for me. Better for them.

It takes forty minutes to locate their position. Two men, camped in a small clearing, but the setup tells me everything I need to know. Thermal blankets instead of a fire, satellite comms, night vision gear—weapons that don't belong in civilian hands.

Private military, or something worse.

I settle into a natural depression thirty yards downwind, draw a handful of pine needles over my boots to dampen my scent. Alpha senses are sharp, but these woods are thick with competing smells. They won't detect me if I stay disciplined.

"Base wants an update," the taller one says, adjusting something on his radio. His partner grunts, cleaning a sidearm with efficiency.

"Tell them we've got sign. Fresh. She's moving northeast, keeping to rough ground."

"She's been out here three weeks. Impressive for an omega."

The second man snorts. "That's why she's worth so much. Client doesn't want some whimpering bitch that'll break in a week."

My fingers dig into the earth. I force my breathing to remain steady, my muscles relaxed. Getting angry would be a luxury I can't afford.

"What's the client paying, anyway?" the first man asks.

"Three times standard. Plus bonus if she's delivered undamaged. Client's geneticist flagged something in her bloodwork—rare compatibility markers, one in ten thousand. The kind of profile he's been hunting for years." He reassembles the gun with a sharp click. "Guy keeps her intake photo framed on his desk. Not in the case file—framed. Like a fucking wedding portrait."

"Though after the trouble she's caused, I'm thinking she needs some attitude adjustment first."

"Boss said no marks."

I swallow bile. These aren't just trackers. They're the worst kind of predators, the kind that enjoy the hunt too much. The kind that consider omegas objects to be used, broken, traded.

Their radio crackles. A third voice, authoritative, impatient. "Status report."

"On her trail, sir. Moving to intercept. Estimate contact within 36 hours."

"Expedite. The buyer is getting impatient. He's arrived personally to oversee transfer."

The men exchange glances. The taller one clears his throat. "Sir, the buyer is on–site? That's unusual protocol."

"This acquisition is priority level alpha. Highest value target we've moved in six months. He's not taking chances after the northern interference with our last shipment. And between us—this one's personal for him. He's been tracking her genetic profile since before we acquired her. Obsessive doesn't begin to cover it."

Northern interference. Jake's words echo in my mind. *There are places, farther north. They handle situations like this... differently.*

"Understood," the man replies. "Do we have a description of potential interferents?"

"Negative. Just be aware this route has had problems. Shipments disappearing. Teams not reporting back. The client believes there's organized resistance targeting our operation."

"Resistance?" The second man scoffs. "It's just omegas running scared."

"Not according to intelligence. These are professionals. Possibly ex-military. They acquire our merchandise and make it disappear."

Make it disappear. To where?

"We'll keep alert," the first man assures. "But we're closing in on the target. Her trail's clear now."

Everything in me goes still. They've found her true path, not the false trails. They're closing in.

"Good. The client wants her secured by tomorrow night. He has a transport waiting to move her across the border immediately. Northern facilities are better equipped for breaking difficult merchandise."

The radio clicks off. The men return to their preparations, checking weapons, studying maps marked with coordinates that are far too close to where I left Sienna's trail. They move with the loose ease of predators who know their prey is cornered.

They won't be the first hunters I've disappointed.

I withdraw as silently as I arrived, circling wide before cutting back toward Sienna's actual trail. My mind catalogs options, discarding each as too risky. If I continue tracking her, I risk leading them straight to her. If I abandon the hunt, they'll find her anyway.

That leaves only one choice.

I move three miles east, to where I know Sienna's false trail begins, and start laying sign. Obvious sign. A broken branch here. A footprint pressed deeper there. A scrap of fabric caught on thorns that matches what she might wear. An abandoned campsite with embers still warm. Each piece of false evidence is a small betrayal of the contract in my pocket—and each one feels more right than the last.

Twenty minutes later, voices drift through the trees. They've taken the bait. I circle behind them, tracking the trackers now, waiting for my moment. It comes when they split up to investigate the campsite, one moving toward the stream, the other examining the fire pit.

The first one never hears me coming.

I strike from behind, arm locked around his throat, cutting off blood flow to his brain. He struggles, but I've done this before. Know exactly how much pressure to apply, how long to hold. His consciousness slips away in seconds. I lower him quietly, zip-tie his hands and feet, and move toward his partner.

This one's more alert, sensing something wrong when his teammate doesn't respond to his call. His hand moves toward his weapon. I don't give him the chance to draw it.

The fight is quick, brutal. He lands one solid blow to my ribs before my fist connects with his jaw. He staggers back. I sweep his legs from under him. His head cracks against stone—not hard enough to kill, just enough to daze. I disarm him, secure him like his partner.

Both unconscious, but alive.

I rifle through their gear, confirming what I suspected. These aren't just traffickers—they're part of something larger, more organized. Their tablets contain encrypted files, most locked behind security I can't bypass. But one document is accessible—a transport manifest with Sienna's description, status, and value.

I have to look away from the number.

The warning about northern interference is there too, highlighted in red:

AVOID NORTHERN CORRIDOR ROUTES. SUSPECTED OMEGA UNDERGROUND NETWORK ACTIVE IN REGIONS 7 AND 8.

Underground network. A margin note in cramped handwriting read,

SETTLEMENT CONFIRMED—SMOKE FROM CHIMNEYS, CULTIVATED LAND, NO REGISTERED INHABITANTS.

It hits me then—the realization of what Jake was hinting at, what these men fear. There are people fighting back. Not just running—building something. Somewhere real.

I stare at the unconscious men, at their weapons, at the coordinates marking Sienna's position. My job was simple: find the missing omega, bring her back to safety. Collect payment. Move on.

But what is safety now? Return her to a system that couldn't protect her the first time? A system where creatures like these operate with impunity?

I gather what I need from their supplies—extra ammunition, first aid kit, their satellite phone, a tactical earpiece still tuned to their comm frequency. I disable their weapons, their radio, their vehicle half-hidden a mile east. Both still breathing. I don't kill anymore.

I pull the sheriff's advance envelope from my pocket, turn it over once, then stuff it deep into a pouch I won't reach for again. This isn't retrieval anymore. It's rescue. And if the buyer is as determined as these men suggest, what comes next won't be easy.

Something I locked down after my last failed rescue cracks loose inside my chest. I let it.

4

SIENNA

I see the whole thing from my perch in the oak's upper branches. The alpha—my tracker—moving with lethal purpose through the underbrush, setting a false trail, then circling back like a predator. Only he's not hunting me. He's hunting them. The men who've been closing in, the ones with military gear and dead eyes. When he takes the first one down, the violence carries years—every strike landing clean, nothing wasted.

The second one doesn't go down as easily. They struggle, a quick blur of fists and grunts. My tracker takes a hit to the ribs that makes me wince, but he doesn't falter. The trafficker's head cracks against stone, and then it's over. My tracker binds both men, rifles through their gear, and disappears back into the forest with purpose in his stride.

I wait ten minutes, letting my racing heart settle. Those men weren't random bounty hunters. I recognize their type from the transport—elite contractors, the kind who enjoy hurting omegas who resist. The kind who leave marks where no one will see them.

My tracker just took them out to protect me.

Unless this is a play to gain my trust. Unless he works for a different buyer.

I need to move. Now.

Descending from the oak is harder than climbing up was. My muscles shake with exhaustion, my hands stiff from gripping branches all day. I misjudge the distance to a lower limb, my foot slipping on wet bark. My ankle twists, catching briefly in a fork of branches before I fall the last eight feet to the ground.

I land hard, biting my lip bloody to keep from crying out. The ankle is already swelling—a deep, sick throb that sharpens with every heartbeat. I probe it gingerly—not broken, but a bad sprain. The kind that needs rest, elevation, ice. None of which I can afford.

"Shit," I hiss through clenched teeth. "Shit, shit, shit."

I drag myself to my feet, testing weight on the injured ankle. It buckles immediately. I catch myself against the tree trunk, swallowing nausea. This is bad. This is survival-threatening bad.

No running now. No climbing. No quick escapes.

I run the math. I have maybe two days of food left. Can't hunt effectively. Can't cover ground.

Can't climb to safe sleeping spots. With those traffickers' colleagues surely on their way, my chances alone have just plummeted from slim to nearly zero.

Which leaves the tracker.

He took out two armed men to protect me. Laid false trails to lead them away. Didn't kill when he could have.

But trusting an alpha—any alpha—goes against every hard-learned lesson of my life.

I hobble painfully to a fallen log, dragging branches to create minimal cover. My water bottle is nearly empty. The forest that's been my refuge for weeks suddenly feels hostile. Exposed. Night will come soon. With it, predators—both animal and human.

Twenty minutes later, I hear him.

Soft footsteps, deliberate enough that I know he wants me to hear his approach. A courtesy. Or a trap. I grip my small knife, knowing it's useless against his training but unwilling to face whatever comes without some defense.

He appears at the edge of the small clearing, tall figure backlit by the setting sun. He stops, hands visible at his sides, giving me space. Giving me choice.

His throat works—a visible swallow, jaw flexing—and I brace for the Voice, the low harmonic that turns resistance to water. It doesn't come. When he speaks, the tone is deliberately flat, stripped of everything an alpha could use to make the words land as command instead of offer.

That, more than anything, makes my decision.

"I know you're hurt," he says. "I can help."

"Why should I trust you?" The words scrape my dry throat.

"You shouldn't." A simple answer. Honest. "But those men aren't the only ones looking for you. And you can't run on that ankle."

I laugh, a harsh sound with no humor. "So either I trust you or I get caught. Some choice."

"There's always choice." He stays where he is, not advancing. "Even bad options are still options."

I study him, this alpha who moves like death but speaks like someone who understands what it means to be cornered. His eyes hold mine steadily, no dominance display, no alpha posturing.

"If I go with you," I say, "I have terms. Non-negotiable."

His eyebrow lifts slightly. "I'm listening."

"No ownership. No alpha commands. No using your voice on me." I lean forward, each word a bullet. "And no lies. You tell me exactly what you know, who sent you, and what you plan to do. The minute you break any of these, I'm gone—bad ankle or not."

He nods once. "Agreed."

The simple acceptance throws me. "Just like that?"

"Just like that." He shifts his weight, wincing slightly. The trafficker's blow to his ribs wasn't as inconsequential as it appeared. "My name is Callan Hodge. Sheriff Rawlins hired me to find you. Those men work for a trafficking ring with a specific buyer waiting for you. They have reinforcements coming. We need to move before they realize their team is down."

Direct. No embellishment. No reassurances.

I want to believe him. That's what makes me wary.

"Who's this buyer?" I ask.

"Don't know his name. Just that he's here personally. And that your value is…" He hesitates.

"Tell me."

"High enough that they're taking extraordinary measures. They never send buyers into the field."

My throat tightens. I remember fragments from the van. Whispered conversation between guards. *Special order. Custom requirements. High-yield merchandise.*

"Let me see your ankle," he says, interrupting my thoughts.

I tense. "Don't touch me."

"I won't. Not without asking." He approaches slowly, then crouches a few feet away, respecting the boundary. "But I need to assess the damage if we're going to cover ground."

I hesitate, then extend my leg slightly. "Look, don't touch."

He studies the swelling. "Bad sprain. You won't be walking far on that." His eyes lift to mine. "May I?" He gestures toward my ankle, hands still not making contact.

I nod once, bracing for pain.

His touch is light, nothing like what I feared. Fingers probe the swelling, testing range without forcing. A medic's hands—but warmth bleeds from the contact point up through my calf, my thigh, settling somewhere it shouldn't. I hold very still.

"We need to bind it," he says, reaching for his pack. "Then find shelter. Those men will be missed soon."

I watch him pull a first aid kit, lay out supplies. He moves where I can see him, telegraphing every reach. No sudden gestures. No looming.

"Why are you doing this?" I ask abruptly. "Sheriff Rawlins can't be paying you enough to take on a trafficking ring."

His hands pause briefly. His expression shifts—old pain, there and gone.

"Not everything is about payment," he says finally.

"Everything is about payment," I counter. "Different currencies, maybe, but nobody does anything for free."

He meets my eyes then, and there's something in his gaze I can't decipher. Something sharper than pity.

"Then consider this payment for services rendered," he says. "You've survived three weeks in wilderness that kills experienced hikers. You've outmaneuvered professional trackers. You've shown more ingenuity than most military-trained personnel I've tracked." He gestures to my ankle. "May I wrap this now?"

Something in his voice lands harder than it should—drops into my chest and sits there, warm and heavy. I nod, watching as he binds my ankle. His thumb brushes the arch of my foot as he finishes, and I forget to breathe for a full second. Snug without squeezing.

"Can you stand?" he asks when he's finished.

I grip the log and push myself upright, testing the wrapped ankle. Still painful, but the support helps. "I can move. Not fast."

"Fast enough." He shoulders his pack, then mine. "We need to reach shelter before dark. There's a cabin about three miles north."

North. The word echoes in my mind. *If you get the chance, run north.*

I study him once more, this alpha who fights like a predator but treats me like an equal. Who asks permission. Who sees my strength instead of my designation.

Still don't trust him. Can't afford to. But for now, he's the only path forward that doesn't end in a cage.

"Lead the way," I say. "But remember my terms."

"No ownership. No commands. No lies." He nods once. "You have my word."

Words are cheap. But as I limp forward, accepting his offered arm only when a fallen log proves impossible to navigate alone, I wonder what currency this alpha truly trades in.

5

—·—

CALLAN

The cabin sits nestled in a fold of mountain ridge most maps don't show. Good. Three miles of punishing terrain with an injured omega means six hours of hypervigilance, of scanning for threats, of listening to Sienna's breathing grow more labored even as she refuses to complain. She only accepts my help over the worst obstacles, her face tight with pain but determined. When the rough-hewn logs finally appear through the trees, relief hits me so hard I almost stumble. Nobody knows about this place except me and the old hunter who died here two winters back. Not on any registry. Not in any database. For the first time in days, I allow myself to think we might actually have a chance.

"There's a creek crossing ahead," I say, pausing to let Sienna catch her breath. Her face is pale, sweat beading despite the cool air. The ankle's worse than she's letting on. "The stones are slick. I need to carry you across."

Her jaw tightens. I see the refusal building before she speaks.

"You can say no," I add quietly. "But there's no shame in accepting help that's freely given."

Something flickers in her eyes—wariness, calculation, maybe a trace of surprise. She studies me for a long moment.

"Ask properly," she says finally.

I understand what she needs—not just help, but control over how it's given. "Sienna, may I carry you across the creek?"

She nods once. "Yes."

I approach slowly, telegraphing my movements. "Arms around my neck. I'll lift on three." Her scent hits me as I bend—wild herbs and pine, undercut with the metallic edge of pain—and desire slams through me so fast I nearly stumble. Not now. Not like this. Something primal stirs in my chest, deeper than the instinct to protect. I lock it down so hard my teeth ache.

She weighs almost nothing in my arms, all wiry muscle and stubborn survival. I feel her tension, the rigid control she maintains even now, refusing to relax against me—and the places where she can't help it, her fingers curling into my collar, her breath warm against my neck. My skin burns everywhere she touches. I carry her exactly as promised, set her down the moment we reach the other side, and my arms feel wrong without her in them.

"Thank you," she says stiffly.

"You're welcome."

The cabin door creaks open to musty darkness. I scan the interior before allowing Sienna to enter, checking corners, closets, the small loft. Old habit. Good habit.

"Wait here," I tell her, helping her to a chair. "I need to secure the perimeter."

I set trip lines, noise traps, map three escape routes. When I return, Sienna hasn't moved from the chair, though her eyes have mapped every inch of the cabin. Survivor's assessment.

"It's secure," I tell her. "For now."

She nods, that sharp gaze fixed on me. "Your ribs. How bad?"

The question surprises me. Most people in her situation wouldn't notice, wouldn't care. "Bruised, not broken. I've had worse."

"Let me see that ankle properly," I say, kneeling before her with the expanded first aid kit from the cabin's stores. "May I remove your boot?"

Another tight nod. I ease the swollen foot free. She hisses once, the only sign of pain she allows. The bruising looks worse now—deep purple spreading across pale skin.

"I need to clean it, reapply a proper wrap. There's ibuprofen for the swelling." I look up, meeting her eyes. "It's going to hurt."

"Just do it," she says.

I clean first, then wrap with steady hands. Her skin is fever-hot against my fingers, but she makes no sound. Only the tension in her body betrays the pain.

"You've done this before," she observes.

"Many times." I secure the last of the wrapping.

"Military?"

"No." I don't elaborate. She doesn't ask. The boundaries between us are clear, necessary.

After, I build a fire in the small woodstove, heat water for coffee and the simple provisions I've carried—dried soup, jerky, a few protein bars. Nothing fancy, but hot food after days in the cold. I place her portion on the small table, then step back, giving her space to eat without feeling crowded.

She watches me move around the cabin, tracking my position even as she eats. Smart. I respect the vigilance, the refusal to let down her guard completely. I'd do the same.

"Why did the sheriff hire you?" she asks abruptly.

I pause, considering my answer. No lies, I'd promised. "Because I find people who don't want to be found. And because I don't ask questions about what happens after."

"But you're asking questions now."

"Yes."

"Why?"

I meet her gaze steadily. "Because those men aren't local law enforcement retrieving a runaway. They're international traffickers retrieving merchandise."

Her spoon clatters against the bowl. "And what does Sheriff Rawlins want with me?"

"Protection, he says."

"You don't believe him?"

"I believe he thinks he can protect you. I'm not convinced the system can."

"The system." She laughs, a brittle sound. "The system is what failed when I was taken from that bus station. The system is what looks the other way when omegas disappear."

"Some parts, yes."

"And Rawlins is different?"

I consider this, choosing my words. "He tries to be. But his jurisdiction has limits. His authority has limits."

"And your authority?" she challenges.

"I have none. Just skills and determination."

Wind moans around the cabin's corners. Rain follows, pattering against the roof, then intensifying to a steady drumbeat. Storm moving in faster than expected. The wilderness making decisions for us.

"We'll need to stay through tomorrow," I say. "That ankle needs rest, and the storm will cover our scent, our tracks."

She nods, eyes fixed on the fire flickering through the woodstove's grate. "What happens after that?"

"That depends."

"On what?"

"On what you want."

Her head snaps up, suspicion evident. "What I want doesn't usually factor into alpha calculations."

"I'm not most alphas."

She shifts in her chair, wincing slightly. "But the law has limits, you say. Protection has limits. So what's the alternative?"

I think of the traffickers' notes. Northern interference. Places beyond reach.

"There are options beyond what the system offers," I say. "People who don't wait for permission to protect."

The fire pops, sending sparks against the grate. Outside, the storm intensifies, rain becoming a roar against the roof. We're trapped here tonight, in this small space that suddenly feels smaller.

Her scent is stronger now in the cabin's confines—woodsmoke and rain sharpened by the omega notes of healing. My hands tighten on the armrest.

"I should check the fire," I say, my voice rougher than intended.

She nods, shifting her injured leg to give me space to pass. The cabin creaks around us, old wood settling in the damp. I kneel before the woodstove, add another log, adjust the damper. Simple actions to focus on, to ground myself against the pull I feel toward her.

I don't realize she's leaned forward until our hands brush—accidental, momentary—as she reaches to steady herself. The contact jolts up my arm like a live wire. Her scent spikes—sharp lemon cutting through woodsmoke—and the alpha in me locks on, a deep pull that floods my senses and coils tight in my gut. Her sharp intake of breath tells me she felt the omega answer to whatever just surged between us. Neither of us moves. The air between our fingers hums.

Our eyes meet for one suspended moment. Something dangerous flickers there.

I withdraw first, standing abruptly. "You should rest. Take the bed. I'll keep watch."

She doesn't argue, just nods once and leverages herself up, careful to avoid my offered hand. The distance reasserts itself between us. Necessary. Safer than the alternative.

But as she limps toward the small bedroom and I settle into the chair by the window, I can still feel the ghost of that touch lingering on my skin. A warning. A reminder of all the ways this mission has already veered beyond my control.

Outside, the storm rages. Inside, the cabin has grown too small for the silence between us.

6

—·—

SIENNA

Three days, and my ankle no longer screams when I put weight on it. The swelling has retreated, leaving behind a watercolor of yellow-green bruising that looks worse than it feels.

We fall into a routine that feels strangely domestic for two people who barely know each other. Mornings for healing and planning. Afternoons for learning.

"Your snares are good," Callan says, examining the simple trap I've constructed from paracord and whittled sticks. "But if you angle the trigger like this—" He adjusts my work with deft fingers, "—it's more sensitive. Less chance of a partial trigger that warns the prey."

I watch his hands, noting how little he wastes—no extra motion, no stray gesture. Like he's spent a lifetime deciding exactly how much of himself to show.

"Where did you learn this?" I ask.

"My grandfather. He was Arapaho. Believed in knowing the land—how to read it, how to live from it."

A fragment. One of the few personal details he's offered.

At night, we take turns keeping watch. The traffickers haven't found us yet, but we both know it's only a matter of time before they expand their search grid this far. Better to stay vigilant than be surprised.

Tonight is different, though. The temperature has dropped sharply, bringing the kind of bone-deep cold that steals breath. I wrap my blanket tighter around my shoulders, watching Callan stoke the fire higher than our usual careful minimum.

"We can risk the extra heat tonight," he says, reading my question before I ask it. "Storm's moving in. It'll mask the smoke."

I nod, huddling closer to the warmth. He settles on the floor nearby, back against the wall, eyes on the window. Always watching. Always ready.

"You've been running a long time," I say, the words slipping out before I can reconsider.

His gaze flicks to mine, then back to the window. "What makes you say that?"

"The way you move. Like you've forgotten how to be still."

A muscle in his jaw tightens, then releases. "Stillness gets people killed."

"Or saved."

"Not in my experience."

The fire crackles between us, sparks dancing up the chimney. Outside, wind moans through pine branches, promising snow by morning.

"What happened?" I ask. "The thing that keeps you running."

He's silent so long I think he won't answer. Then, quietly: "I was hired to extract a family. Omega mother, two young children. Abusive alpha husband with political connections."

"Political connections." The words taste familiar. The kind that make difficult daughters disappear into systems designed to break them.

His eyes never leave the window, but I can tell he's seeing something else entirely. "I got them out. Had them in a safe house upstate. Twenty-four hours from the border. I left to secure transportation. Two hours. That's all."

"And he found them."

Callan's jaw tightens. "Used his voice on the oldest boy. Made him unlock the door."

My stomach clenches. Alpha voice. Three years in a rehabilitation center taught me what comes after.

"The mother fought," he continues. "Got one child out through a window. The other..." He shakes his head. "I was too late. By minutes."

The weight of his failure sits heavy in the small cabin. I understand it. The inside of it.

"My parents sold me when I was sixteen," I say. Not planned. The words just surface, pulled loose by his honesty. "A rehabilitation center for difficult omegas. Three years before I found a way out."

His head turns sharply. I keep my eyes on the fire.

"You were a child," he says, voice rough.

"I was an omega. That's all that mattered." The bitterness bleeds through despite my effort to sound matter-of-fact. "Spent five years after that working under the table. Sleeping in shelters. Never staying anywhere long enough to be registered."

"Until Portland."

"Until Portland." I close my eyes briefly. "One mistake. Got on the wrong bus. Or the right one, for them."

Embers shift and settle in the grate. We sit with each other's pain, neither trying to fix or minimize.

"The ones who got away," I say finally. "The mother and child."

Something shifts in his expression. "Safe. Beyond reach."

"Beyond reach," I echo. The phrase settles between us.

"You haven't asked what happens if Rawlins finds us," Callan says.

"Don't need to. I know the protocol. Safe house. Testimony. Witness protection, maybe, if I'm lucky. A new identity that still marks me as unclaimed omega. Just another kind of cage."

His silence is confirmation enough.

Outside, the wind howls louder. Snow begins to patter against the windows, soft at first, then more insistent. Callan rises, checks the locks, scans the perimeter through frosted glass.

"Storm's worse than expected," he says. "We'll need to extend our stay another day at least."

I nod, watching him return to his position against the wall. His jaw is tight, shoulders hunched slightly against the cold that seeps through the old cabin's bones. He won't complain. Won't ask for comfort.

Making my decision, I unfold myself from my spot by the fire and move toward him. He watches, wary, as I settle beside him, close enough that our shoulders almost touch.

"What are you doing?" he asks.

I unfurl my blanket, offering half. "It's cold. Shared body heat is more efficient."

He hesitates, eyes searching mine for the catch, the angle, the hidden expectation.

"Just warmth," I say. "Nothing more."

After another moment, he nods, accepting the offered corner of blanket. We sit side by side, not quite touching, wrapped in shared warmth. The inch between his shoulder and mine feels electric—a gap I'm acutely, stupidly aware of with every breath. The simple act feels monumental—the first time in weeks, maybe years, I've willingly moved closer to an alpha rather than away.

"Thank you," he says, so quietly I almost miss it.

I don't reply. Don't need to. We watch the storm together, this strange alliance of two scarred people who've spent too long running alone. His breathing eventually steadies into the rhythm of someone accustomed to finding rest in small moments. Not sleep—he's too vigilant for that—but a rare lowering of defenses.

It's a small thing, this shared blanket. Insignificant against the backdrop of traffickers and wilderness and uncertain futures. But as the night deepens around us and the fire burns low, his scent wraps around me as surely as the wool—pine and smoke and clean skin—and my body hums with the nearness of him, a low current I couldn't shut off if I tried. I recognize this for what it is—the first thing either of us has built that isn't a defense.

7

—·—

CALLAN

I find the first drone at dawn, tangled in pine branches half a mile west of the cabin. Military-grade, compact, thermal imaging capable. I disable it, hands working from memory—twist, pull, disconnect—then bury the pieces in separate locations. Bad luck for them, finding it like this. Worse luck for us, that they've brought this level of tech to the hunt. I scan the sky, aware of how exposed I am on this ridge. They're not just tracking anymore. They're hunting with intent, with resources, with desperation. Desperate predators don't follow patterns.

Two hours into my scouting circuit, I find worse. Boot prints from three different men moving in a coordinated grid—elite trackers, former special forces maybe, the kind who rarely leave witnesses. A communications relay hidden in brush a mile east confirms it: they're not just hunting. They're building infrastructure. The earpiece crackles—a handler's voice, clipped and impatient. *Team Bravo is dark. All units collapse to sector seven. Converge on the northeast corridor.* A second handler cuts in. *Remind all units—the client carries federal liaison credentials. Any local law contact, defer to his authority. Jurisdictional courtesy is already on file with the regional office.* Four callsigns acknowledge in rapid succession. They've absorbed the loss and redeployed within hours.

By midday, I've found their base camp three miles from the cabin. Four men, heavily armed, operating with military discipline.

Their conversation drifts up the ridge in fragments.

"...expected extraction window closing..."

"...client growing impatient..."

"...highest priority acquisition this year..."

One man gestures to a black SUV parked at the edge of camp. The windows are tinted, but I catch movement inside—someone watching, someone directing. Not out in the field with the others. Someone who considers themselves above the dirty work.

The buyer himself. It hits me with cold certainty. Buyers never come to the field. They wait in clean, climate-controlled rooms for their merchandise to be delivered. They don't risk exposure, don't get their hands dirty with the ugly reality of what they purchase.

Unless the stakes are extraordinarily high.

One of the men approaches the SUV, stands at rigid attention while the rear window lowers slightly. I can't see the face, can't hear the exchange. But the man's posture tells me everything—whoever sits in that vehicle holds power. Absolute power.

When he returns to the others, his demeanor has changed. Tenser. More urgent.

"New orders. The client wants her secured by tomorrow night, whatever it takes. The last transport window closes at 0600."

"What about the interference reported by Team Bravo?"

"Neutralize with extreme prejudice. No witnesses."

My blood runs cold. Team Bravo—the men I disabled. They've been found, reported back. And now anyone helping Sienna is marked for death.

I withdraw, using every skill I've built through years of tracking to move without leaving sign. At the ridgeline I stop, pressing my back against cold granite, and let the shift happen—the quiet click from observer to combatant. My breathing slows. The forest sharpens into vectors and sightlines, every tree becoming cover or obstacle, every shadow a potential firing position. Only when the calculation settles, clean and certain, do I start moving again.

By the time I circle back toward the cabin, I've identified our only viable escape route—a narrow corridor to the northeast that their search pattern hasn't yet covered. It won't stay open long.

I pause at the ridgeline, studying the terrain below. The route I've identified leads eventually toward Rawlins' jurisdiction. Not safety, exactly, but temporary shelter. Enough for Sienna to catch her breath, decide her next move.

Getting Sienna through that corridor safely will require a diversion—someone drawing pursuit west while she moves northeast. The tactical math is simple. The weight in my chest when I run it is not.

I make my way back to the cabin, approaching from downwind to ensure no scent trail leads directly to our location. Through the dirty window, I catch glimpses of her moving inside—checking supplies, testing her weight on the healing ankle, scanning her surroundings the way she scans everything—like the walls might move.

The small scar at the corner of her mouth deepens as she concentrates on the repaired snare, testing each knot. The same hands that fisted my hair hours ago move with surgical precision now, and something low in my gut tightens at the dissonance—how those fingers felt twisted against my scalp versus how they look testing paracord knots. My body remembers before my brain can intervene, and I have to look away.

The image arrives without permission—morning light through a kitchen window, her hands wrapped around a mug instead of paracord, no rifles propped by the door. A table with nothing on it but coffee and the unhurried quiet of a life I stopped imagining years ago.

I blink it gone. The afterimage clings like woodsmoke. Somewhere north, if the intel is real, people have built exactly that—ordinary mornings behind walls no one can breach. The thought cracks something I've kept sealed since the safe house: the belief that wanting a life like that is what gets people killed.

I focus on practical considerations. How to present the plan. How to ensure she reaches Rawlins safely. How to create a diversion convincing enough to draw all pursuit away from her path.

Her scent clings to my jacket collar—lemon and woodsmoke, faint but unmistakable. My hand drifts toward the fabric, thumb rubbing the weave where her hair brushed it, and heat blooms in my chest before I catch myself and force my hand back to the rifle stock.

That reflex has no place in what comes next.

I check my weapons one last time before approaching the cabin. The rifle. The sidearm. The knife at my ankle. Tools of a trade I've practiced too long to question now.

The plan locks into place. Get her to Rawlins. Lead the hunters away. Give her the chance to decide her own fate, even if I won't be there to see what she chooses.

It has to be.

I take one last look at the wilderness stretching in all directions, at the vastness that has been both my refuge and my prison for so many years. Then I turn toward the cabin, toward the woman whose freedom has somehow become more important than my survival.

Toward whatever comes next.

I approach the cabin slowly, careful not to broadcast my presence until I've confirmed Sienna is alone. Through the window I watch her move—counting cans, testing zippers, weighing what stays and what gets left behind. Even favoring the bad ankle, she's coiled tight, ready to bolt the second I give the word. Part of me wants to tell her she's the most capable person I've tracked in years. I don't. We're down to odds and ends and the next three hours, maximum, before the search grid closes in.

She registers my shadow through the glass, and instead of panic, I see something like focus sharpen her features. She meets me at the door, jaw set. "They're closer?"

I nod, stepping inside. The smell of smoke and melting snow clings to her. "We go in ten. Bring only what you can carry at a dead sprint."

She doesn't waste time questioning, just grabs her pack, slings it tight, and kills the fire fast, no wasted motion.

She follows me into the predawn dark. Doesn't look back. I take point, moving fast and low, keeping to the game trails where the snow is thinnest. She matches pace, her breathing audible but controlled, her ankle showing only as a hitch in her stride every few steps. Good. If she can keep up now, she can manage the full run when it matters.

For the first half mile—boots on frozen duff, wind through the pines. Then a high-pitched whirr cuts the air overhead. Sienna tenses but doesn't break stride.

"Drone," she whispers. "Thermal?"

"Probably," I reply. "Stay under the trees. If I say down, drop and don't move."

She nods, teeth glinting in the moonlight.

We press on, accelerating through a narrow ravine that acts as a blind spot for aerial surveillance. I know these woods better than anyone breathing, but the drone is patient—circling just outside visual range, never out of earshot. They're herding us toward the only exit they've left unmonitored. I file it away for later, if there is one.

At the two-mile mark, my inner clock tells me we're ahead of the search parties. I glance at Sienna. Face flushed, sweat at her temple despite the cold, jaw locked on whatever pain she's swallowing. She doesn't flag.

The drone drops lower, sound swelling. I signal stop and she drops with me into the hollow beneath a massive fallen spruce. Decades of rot and snowmelt have carved out the trunk—barely enough space for two bodies chest to back, faces pressed to the forest floor.

I wedge myself behind her, arm braced over her head to prevent the drone's camera from catching a glimpse of exposed skin. Sienna's back meets my chest and every nerve in my body fires at once. Her scent floods the tight space—sharp and close, lemon and heat and omega—and my hips jerk involuntarily before I lock them still. Adrenaline. Just adrenaline.

Above, the drone hovers, the sound vibrating through the wood. Sienna turns her head, voice a whisper against my bicep. "Is this really the best spot?"

"It's the only spot," I murmur.

She shivers, not from cold. My hand, still caging her head, ends up tangled in her hair, and for a moment, all I can think of is the way her pulse pounds quick and strong beneath my palm.

The drone lingers, then veers west. We don't move. Her breath slows. The rigid line of her spine softens into something else.

"How long do we wait?" she asks, voice barely audible. Her lips move against my bicep, and the sensation arrows straight down my spine.

"As long as it takes."

And if she presses back against me, just a fraction deeper—her hips shifting, fitting against mine in a way that makes my vision blur—I don't stop her.

8

SIENNA

Pressed against Callan in the narrow hollow beneath ancient tree roots, I count heartbeats instead of seconds. One-two-three-four. His chest rises and falls against my back in controlled, silent breathing. One-two-three-four. Outside our hiding place, boots crush fallen leaves, voices murmur terse commands. The buyer's men, close enough that I can smell gun oil and the artificial tang of scent suppressants. One-two-three-four. Callan's hand rests lightly on my shoulder, neither restraining nor commanding—just present, a reminder that I'm not facing this alone. Not yet, anyway.

We'd almost walked right into them. Patrol appearing around a bend in the trail as we scouted our escape route. No time for planning or discussion—just Callan's hand closing around mine, pulling me toward this hollowed space beneath massive roots, bodies pressed together in breathless silence while death walks ten feet away.

"South quadrant clear," a voice announces. "Moving to checkpoint delta."

Footsteps recede. Neither of us moves, trained by survival to wait until certainty replaces probability. Minutes pass, stretching into an hour. My cramped muscles protest, but the discomfort barely registers against the question I've been circling all day.

Soon, I'll have to decide. Stay with the alpha who's kept me alive, or strike out alone again. Three weeks taught me self-reliance, but also its limits.

"They're gone," Callan whispers, his breath warm against my ear. "But we should wait another hour before moving."

I nod, shifting slightly to ease the pressure on my healing ankle. The movement presses me more firmly against him, and I feel the immediate tension in his body—the careful restraint as he tries to give me what space he can in our confined shelter.

Asking, never taking.

I run the count without meaning to. The carving replaced beneath its rock instead of pocketed as evidence. Every touch preceded by a question. The terms he accepted without negotiation—no ownership, no commands, no voice. My body keeps its own tally underneath: his scent never spikes with aggression, my pulse settles instead of climbs when he's near, the omega pull I keep *choosing* to follow rather than fighting to resist.

The math shouldn't add up. It does.

"Tell me about the northern territories," I say, voice barely audible. The question has lingered since I first heard him mention them.

He's silent so long I think he won't answer. Then, barely audible: "Places beyond typical jurisdiction. Full omega autonomy. No registration, no forced pairing."

"That's not possible."

"I've seen evidence. Omegas who vanished from the system. Traffickers who went north and never came back."

"The woman in the transport van," I murmur. "She said there were riders."

His body stills against mine. "When we get out of here, I can help you find those connections."

We. Get you. The subtle distinction in his words doesn't escape me.

"You're not coming," I say. Not a question.

"My job is to get you to safety."

"And then what?"

The question hangs between us, too honest for the careful distance we've maintained.

"I've lost people I was supposed to protect," he says finally. "Staying makes that worse."

"For who?"

He doesn't answer, but I feel the truth in the tension of his body against mine. Safer for him. Safer than risking another failure.

Darkness deepens around us as the sun sets. In our hidden hollow, his scent envelops me—pine and woodsmoke and something uniquely alpha, yet without the aggressive dominance I'm used to from his kind.

"I don't know how to do this," I admit.

His hand finds mine in the darkness, resting alongside. "I understand that better than you might think."

And I believe him.

"Sienna." My name in his voice sounds different in the darkness. A question, not a demand. "May I?"

The ambiguity of the request should frighten me. Instead, I turn within the confined space, facing him though I can barely make out his features in the shadows.

"Yes," I whisper.

His hand lifts slowly, giving me every opportunity to withdraw, and brushes a strand of hair from my face. The touch is feather-light, reverent in its restraint. My breath catches.

"Tell me to stop and I will," he says. "Immediately. No questions."

I nod, not trusting my voice. His fingers trace the line of my jaw, tentative, exploring. I should be planning escape routes, guarding against the moment when gentleness turns to control.

Instead, I lean in—starved for contact that doesn't hurt.

"May I kiss you?" he asks, each word weighed.

"Yes."

His lips meet mine with the same restrained gentleness as his touch, unhurried and simply present. I respond hesitantly—then his scent shifts, deepens, alpha pheromones flooding the small space with something warm and anchoring, and my body answers before my mind catches up. Something old and certain loosens in my chest—not submission, not surrender. Recognition. Want unfurls beneath it, simple and startling.

When we part, his forehead rests against mine, breathing unsteady. "We should stop. Because you're vulnerable—"

I silence him with another kiss. "I've spent my life being told what I can and can't choose. Don't take this choice from me too."

His breath catches. "Sienna, are you sure? Here? Now?"

"I'm sure about now," I say. "Tomorrow has too many variables. But right now, in this moment, I choose this. I choose you."

The darkness around us feels suddenly charged, alive with possibility and danger in equal measure. His hands frame my face with impossible gentleness.

"Tell me what you want," he says. "Exactly what you want."

"Touch me," I breathe. "Just… touch me like I won't break."

His hands start at my shoulders, thumbs tracing the line of my collarbones through thin fabric. "Here?" A question, not a statement. I nod, and his fingers slide lower, skimming the curve of my ribs with a reverence that makes my throat ache. Each touch preceded by a word, a glance, a pause long enough for me to close the distance or pull away.

I close the distance. Every time.

When his mouth finds the hollow of my throat, his scent deepens—pine and alpha musk thickening until the air between us feels like something I could drown in. The omega in me hums with it, an answer rising hot and liquid in my belly, and I arch into him before I can think about why. His breath stutters against my skin.

"More," I say, and it comes out rougher than I intended. "I want more."

He undresses me slowly, hands shaking just enough that I know this costs him something too. When his mouth drops to my breast, tongue circling, teeth grazing, a sound escapes me that I've never made—raw, unguarded. His groan vibrates against my skin in answer, and his scent floods so thick I can taste it, salt-sweet at the back of my tongue.

I pull at his shirt, needing skin against skin, needing to feel the heat of him without barriers. When our chests press together, we both go still—the shock of full contact, of warmth meeting warmth, of his heart hammering against mine. His hand slides down my stomach, fingers hovering at the waistband.

"Yes," I whisper before he can ask. "*Yes.*"

His touch between my thighs is careful, exploratory—learning pressure, rhythm, reading my breath the way he reads trails. When he finds what makes my hips roll, he stays there, patient and relentless, until I'm trembling against him, fingers twisted in his hair, gasping words that aren't quite words.

"I want—" I can barely get the words out, but I need them said. "I need you. Inside me. Now."

The space is so tight the want alone could crush me. My hands scrabble at his shirt, and his body tenses, stutters, like maybe he needs this as badly as I do. His hand, careful and broad, slides from my shoulder to my hip. He shifts, balances his weight above me, and my legs fall open so we fit together, puzzle-tight. The open air between us is measured in inches, then none, as his skin brushes mine.

Every nerve is lit—every cell screaming *yes, yes, now.*

He presses in slowly, as if he can't believe I actually want this from him. Nothing in his face is demanding. Only awe, only the need to be sure. His forehead finds mine, bodies so close I can't tell where I end. The first thrust is slow, cautious, the breadth of him stretching me open in a way that should hurt, but it doesn't. It's pressure, fullness, a heat that builds at the base of my spine and crackles up through every nerve I own.

I gasp—his name, maybe, or just the sound of being filled. His eyes catch the noise, and for a second I think he's going to stop. His lips brush my cheek, my jaw. "Tell me if you want to stop," he breathes.

"Don't. Please don't." I lock my ankles around his hips, anchor myself to the reality of this, of him, and he groans, the sound low and ragged and so intimate it makes my toes curl. He works his way deeper, each inch a negotiation with my body. I give him everything. When he bottoms out, his hips flush against mine, the sensation is so right I almost cry.

He holds still, letting me set the rhythm. "Okay?" he whispers.

"More than okay," I say, and pull him down for a kiss that is all salt and teeth and the taste of wanting. We breathe together through it, and the omega in me rises—not submission, but recognition. *This one. Safe. Mine.*

We move together slowly, deliberately—finding a rhythm that belongs only to this moment, to this hidden place beneath ancient roots. His scent pulses with each thrust, thick and anchoring, and my body answers in kind, slick heat building between us until the friction is devastating. His mouth finds mine, swallowing the sounds I make, giving back his own—low, broken, reverent.

When I shatter, it's with his name on my lips and his arms tight around me, and he follows seconds later, shuddering, face buried in my neck, breathing my name like a prayer he'd forgotten he knew.

After, we lie tangled together in our small shelter, his arms around me, my head on his chest. His heartbeat steady beneath my ear. One-two-three-four. The same rhythm that anchored me when danger passed outside. His fingers trace lazy patterns on my bare shoulder, touch no less reverent now than before.

"You're thinking too loud," he murmurs into my hair.

I smile against his skin. "Just... processing."

"Regrets?"

"No." The certainty in my voice surprises even me. "No regrets."

His arms tighten slightly, a gentle pressure that asks nothing, demands nothing. And in that simple hold, I recognize something I'd dismissed as fantasy—the feeling of safety that comes not from walls or weapons, but from being seen and respected.

Like the whispered stories of sanctuaries where safety isn't conditional.

For the first time, I can almost believe such places exist. The thought terrifies me more than the alternative—because believing means wanting something I might actually get.

A future I might have to face alone, if Callan's earlier words hold true.

I push the thought away, focusing instead on this moment—on warmth and connection in a world that's given me precious little of either. Tomorrow will bring decisions. Dangers. Crossroads. But tonight, in this hidden hollow beneath ancient roots, I allow myself to exist fully in the present.

9

CALLAN

Dawn breaks in shades of steel and smoke. Rain by midday—good. It'll dampen scent, kill drone visibility, wash tracks clean. Intercepted radio chatter confirms what I feared—three patrols now, closing the net. Hours, not days.

I've plotted Sienna's corridor—stream beds and rock outcroppings northeast to Rawlins' jurisdiction. Eight miles. Four hours if her ankle holds. I'd used the satellite phone at first light—Rawlins' voice tight with relief when I confirmed she was alive, tighter when I told him what was closing in. He'll position deputies at the border crossing.

Long enough for me to ensure no one follows.

I haven't told her that part. Haven't explained that the diversion I've planned isn't just a false trail, but a direct confrontation. A one-man stand to occupy every hunter long enough for her to vanish beyond their reach.

She'd refuse to go if she knew. Would insist on finding another way, a way that doesn't split us up. A way that keeps us both alive.

A motel door swings open in my memory—broken hinges, a child's shoe overturned on stained carpet, the smell of alpha rage so thick it coated my tongue for days afterward. Two hours. I'd left them for two hours.

There isn't one.

"The ravine route looks clear," Sienna says, appearing at my shoulder. Her quiet approach still surprises me—most people can't move that silently, especially not in wilderness terrain.

I nod, folding the map to hide the western trails I've marked for myself. "It's our best option. Once you reach this ridge—" I indicate the boundary line, "—you're in Rawlins' territory. He'll have deputies watching the approaches."

"And after that?" She asks the question casually, but I hear the tension beneath.

"Temporary safe house. Time to decide your next move."

"Which is what, exactly? Testify against traffickers who'll never see a courtroom? Enter witness protection as an unclaimed omega, forever marked as vulnerable?"

"Or north," I say quietly. "Rawlins knows people. Connections. The underground network that moves omegas beyond the system's reach."

Her eyes search mine. "You believe it exists now."

"I do."

"But you're not coming."

I look away, focusing on packing essential supplies into her backpack. "My job is to get you safely to Rawlins. What happens after isn't my concern."

What happens to her after has become my only concern—every thought that should be tactical bending toward her instead. I check her provisions—water, food, first aid, her pocket knife. All the while aware of her eyes on me, seeing more than I want her to see.

"That's bullshit," she says finally.

I meet her gaze, keeping my expression neutral. "It's protocol."

"After last night, you're really going with protocol?"

Last night. The bruise on my ribs throbs where she pressed against me, and for a half-second the pain isn't pain—it's the phantom weight of her body, the catch in her breath. I breathe through it the way I'd breathe through a gunshot wound.

"Last night doesn't change the reality of our situation," I say, more harshly than intended.

She flinches, almost imperceptibly, then masks it with a hard smile. "Right. Just survival instincts. Biology. Nothing personal."

"Sienna—"

"Save it." She shoulders her pack, wincing slightly. "I get it. You rescue, you don't stick around. Clean exit. No messy attachments."

Her anger is better than her grief. I let her believe I'm just another alpha who takes what he wants, then walks away.

The rain starts as we make final preparations, fat droplets that quickly become a steady downpour. I check my weapons one last time—rifle, sidearm, the combat knife strapped to my ankle. Tools for what comes next.

"Stay in the tree line as much as possible," I instruct, voice flat. "Use the ravine until you hit the river fork, then follow the eastern bank. There's a rock formation that looks like a wolf's head—Rawlins will be waiting beyond it."

She nods, face set in determined lines. "And where will you be?"

"Creating a diversion." The partial truth. "Drawing attention west while you move east."

"Then meeting me at the rendezvous point."

Not a question. An assumption. My jaw locks.

"If I can," I say, knowing I won't. Knowing that once I engage the buyer's team, there will be no clean exit. No meeting up later. Just buying time with the only currency I have left—myself.

She studies me, eyes narrowing slightly. Reading the lie, or at least suspecting it. I've underestimated her again. She sees too much, knows too much about survival and its costs.

"We go together," she says flatly.

"That's not the plan."

"Fuck the plan." Her voice rises slightly, then she catches herself, glancing toward the window where rain streaks the dirty glass. "We've made it this far by sticking together. Changing that now is tactically unsound."

"It's the only way to ensure you reach Rawlins safely."

"Why? What aren't you telling me?"

The direct question lands. I turn away, checking equipment that's already been checked, buying seconds to compose my response.

"The buyer's men are closing in from three directions," I say finally. "Their focus is capture, not kill—they want you alive. That gives us an advantage, but only if we split their attention."

"So you're what, going to walk right into them? Let yourself be captured?"

"I'm going to ensure you have a clear path." Not a direct lie, but nowhere near the full truth.

She steps closer, her scent sharpening with anger and something else—fear, but not for herself. "And what happens to you when you've ensured that path?"

I meet her gaze steadily. "I handle it. Like I always do."

"That's not an answer."

"It's the only one I have." I zip her pack closed with finality. "We move in twenty minutes. Northeast for you. I'll head west, lay an obvious trail, engage their attention. Once you reach Rawlins, you're beyond their jurisdiction. Beyond their reach."

"And if I refuse to go without you?"

The question hangs between us, heavy with everything these days of shared survival have built.

"Then we both lose," I say. "And everything we've fought for means nothing."

Her expression flattens, the vulnerability gone as fast as it surfaced. She nods once, sharply. "Fine. Your plan. Your rules." She turns away, but not before I catch the flash of hurt in her eyes.

"Twenty minutes."

She moves to the other side of the cabin, checking her own gear with quick, angry movements. I watch her, memorizing details I have no tactical reason to notice—the determined set of her shoulders, the way she tucks stray hair behind her ear with unconscious grace, the quiet competence in her hands.

None of them were Sienna.

Her lemon-sharp scent lingers on my collar. My throat closes around something I can't swallow. I turn away before she can read my face, but my hands betray me—they've stopped moving over the gear, frozen midway through a buckle, shaped around an absence.

Twenty minutes. That's all we have left together. Twenty minutes before we part.

Before I lose the only thing I've wanted to keep.

10

SIENNA

I see it in the way he avoids my eyes, in how he's packed my bag with everything essential while his holds only weapons. Callan isn't planning a diversion. He's planning to sacrifice himself. The bastard is going to lead them away from me, make himself the target, ensure they take him instead of me. And he thought I wouldn't notice. Thought I'd just walk away believing he'd follow later. As if I haven't survived by reading the unspoken, by noticing the smallest tells between words. As if I don't know exactly what martyrdom looks like when it's being packaged as protection.

Anger replaces everything else. I drop my pack to the floor with a thud that makes him turn.

"You're not coming back," I say, voice steady despite the rage boiling beneath. "You never planned to."

His face gives nothing away, but his scent sharpens with surprise, then resignation. "Sienna—"

"Don't." I step closer, fury propelling me forward. "Don't you dare lie to me now. You're planning to die out there."

"Not die. Delay them. Create time for you to—"

"Bullshit." I close the distance. "I saw your pack. Nothing but weapons and ammo. You're going to engage them directly, make sure they focus on you instead of me. Make sure they take you instead."

His jaw tightens. "It's the only way to guarantee you reach Rawlins safely."

"So you decided. Without asking. Without telling me." My hands curl into fists at my sides. "How is that different from what every other alpha has done? Deciding my future without my consent?"

That hits him, I can see it in the flinch he can't quite suppress. "I'm trying to save your life."

"By throwing away yours?" I laugh, a harsh sound that scrapes my throat raw. "That's not salvation, Callan. That's just another kind of cage."

He runs a hand over his face, the first crack in his composed facade. "Those men outside have orders to take you at any cost. The only way to stop them is to give them something they want more."

"And after? After you're captured or killed, what then? I just keep running alone for the rest of my life?"

Something flickers in his eyes—pain, quickly shuttered. "You'll have options. Rawlins knows people. The northern network—"

"I don't want a network." I step closer until we're almost touching. "I want a place where safety isn't something temporary. Where it's ordinary. Shared."

His breathing changes, becomes uneven. "Sienna, I can't—"

"Can't what? Live? Be happy? Choose something beyond sacrifice and penance for whatever happened in your past?"

He looks away, but I catch his chin, force him to meet my gaze. "You talk about giving me choices, but you've already decided your own fate. Already decided you don't deserve to walk out of here with me."

"I don't," he says, so quietly I almost miss it. "Not after—"

"After what? Failing those people years ago? How many have you saved since? How many have you protected, guided, freed?"

"It doesn't erase what happened."

"Nothing will. Ever. But it doesn't mean you're obligated to die to balance some cosmic scale."

The air between us feels electric, charged with anger and fear and something deeper, something neither of us has named. His scent has changed, intensified—alpha notes mingling with something uniquely Callan, a scent that's become safety and warmth and possibility.

"I can't lose you too," he whispers. "If something happens to you because I wasn't good enough, fast enough—"

"Then we face it together," I say. "No more lone wolf bullshit. No more martyrdom disguised as protection. We go together or not at all."

His eyes darken, pupils expanding with emotion too complex to name. We stand frozen, tension holding us both still.

And something shifts in my chest—the same instinct that kept me alive in the wilderness, the fierce animal certainty that you seize what matters before it's ripped away. Not desperation. Decision.

I make the choice for both of us.

Closing the last distance between us, I take his face in my hands and kiss him—not gentle, not tentative, but fierce and demanding and certain. His response is immediate, arms wrapping around me, pulling me against him with a desperation that matches my own. Nothing like our first time—this is claim and counter-claim, demand and answer, fear burned clean.

Clothing becomes an obstacle, discarded with urgent hands. His mouth traces fire down my neck, finding the places he's already learned, and when old habit makes him hesitate, I growl low in my throat and pull him closer.

"Don't you dare hold back now."

Something breaks in him then. He lifts me, my legs wrapping around his waist, back pressed against the rough cabin wall—the wood grain biting into my shoulder blades and I want that too, want every sensation sharp and real. When he enters me it's with a groan that sounds like surrender, one deep stroke that fills me so completely my vision whites at the edges.

"*Fuck*," I breathe, and his hips stutter at the word, his scent crashing over me—no longer restrained, no longer careful, just raw alpha need that makes the omega in me surge to meet it, slick and desperate and *aching*.

I meet him thrust for thrust, nails scoring his back, marking him the way I've chosen to—fiercely, deliberately, with everything I refused to feel before this moment. His mouth drags hot and open across my collarbone, teeth grazing the place where my pulse hammers, and the sound I make is feral, possessive—a claim, not a plea.

His hands grip my hips hard enough to bruise and I want the bruises, want proof that this was real when the adrenaline fades. The angle shifts and I gasp, clenching around him, and his forehead drops to my shoulder with a guttural sound that vibrates through my whole body.

"More," I demand, fisting his hair, pulling his head back so he has to look at me. "Don't stop. Don't you *dare* stop."

He obeys—not in submission, but in answer. Harder. Deeper. Each thrust driving us both toward something inevitable. We move together like the fight we just had—no quarter given, nothing held in reserve. His scent and mine tangle into something new, something that smells like both of us, like belonging.

"I'm here," I tell him when his rhythm turns ragged. "Right here."

His hand slides between us, finding me—he's been paying attention, every time—and the coil in my core snaps so hard I cry out, back arching off the wall, pulling him impossibly deeper. He follows me over with a sound caught between my name and a sob, burying himself to the hilt and holding there, shaking, while the aftershocks roll through us both.

The silence after feels like the forest after a storm. Wrecked and clean and still.

Afterward, he doesn't pull away as I half-expected. Instead, he gathers me closer, his forehead resting against mine, our breathing syncing into a shared rhythm. The frantic edge of fear and desperation gradually fades, replaced by something steadier, more grounded.

"We go together," he says finally, the words rough against my lips.

"Together. Whatever comes."

His arms tighten around me, and I feel the shift—the lone wolf accepting a partner at his side.

When we rise to dress and plan, the rain has stopped. The forest glistens, washed clean, and the path ahead is neither east nor west. Just forward.

11

CALLAN

We move like ghosts through dawn mist, following the narrow ridge between patrols. The earpiece has tracked three formation shifts since we left the cabin—each one tighter, the callsigns multiplying, the buyer's clipped voice surfacing on comms more frequently as he moves his command post closer to the corridor. Sienna matches my pace step for step, no longer the injured omega I found in the wilderness but a partner equally invested in our survival. The weight of her decision—our decision—to face this together sits like armor across my shoulders. Strange how choosing to protect someone who refuses to be left behind feels different than sacrifice. The earpiece I salvaged from the traffickers' gear crackles with fragments of radio chatter. They're mobilizing, converging, sensing we're on the move. The net tightens with each passing minute. But for the first time, I'm not calculating a lone wolf's odds. I'm planning for two to survive.

"They've changed formation," I murmur, helping Sienna navigate a steep slope of loose shale. "Moving to block the eastern approach to the border." A burst of static, then a voice I haven't heard before—clipped, European-accented: *I'm repositioning to the corridor personally. If she reaches the border, we lose her permanently.* The buyer. Moving to intercept us himself.

She nods, face set in determined lines. "Alternative route?"

"Through the ravine. It's narrow, defensible." I don't add the obvious—it's also a potential trap if they're waiting at the other end.

"Then we go through it."

The ravine cuts like an ancient wound through granite hillside, barely wide enough for us to move single file in places. Morning light barely penetrates here, leaving us in blue-gray shadow. Good for concealment. Better for ambush. Every instinct says stop, but the alternatives have narrowed to none.

Halfway through, Sienna freezes, hand raised in warning. I stop instantly, scanning for what triggered her alarm. Nothing visible, no sound beyond the whisper of wind through stone.

Then I catch it—the faintest trace of artificial scent blocker, barely detectable beneath pine and wet stone. Someone's trying very hard not to be smelled. Someone nearby.

"Three o'clock," she breathes, barely audible. "Behind the split boulder."

I nod once, impressed and unsurprised by her perception. She's survived this long because she notices what others miss. I signal our approach—flanking maneuver, my lead. She counters with a different pattern—simultaneous engagement from two sides. Riskier, but potentially more effective.

I hesitate, then nod agreement. Treating her as an equal means accepting her tactical input, not just her presence. We split, moving in opposite directions in silence, converging on the boulder from both sides.

But our quarry is already moving. A figure darts from cover, sprinting toward the ravine's exit. Not a standard patrol member—the build is wrong, the movement too fluid. I give chase, aware of Sienna paralleling on the opposite side.

The figure reaches the ravine's mouth and stops, turning to face us with eerie composure. The mist parts, revealing a man in his fifties, silver-haired, impeccably dressed even in wilderness terrain. Behind him, two guards materialize from concealed positions, weapons raised.

"Fascinating," the man says, voice soft, accent faintly European. His gaze fixes on Sienna with the flat assessment of someone appraising livestock. This isn't just a trafficker. This is the buyer himself.

"Step away from her," I order, rifle trained on his chest.

He doesn't flinch. "Her genetic markers are extraordinarily rare. You understand—this isn't personal. It's procurement."

Sienna's scent sharpens with disgust and rage, but her voice remains steady. "I'm not merchandise."

"No?" He gestures, and four more guards emerge from the tree line. "Then why does everyone keep setting a price?"

I track the guards' positions, calculating angles, cover, odds. Six against two, with the ravine at our backs. Bad positioning. Worse numbers.

"You have two options," the buyer continues smoothly. "Surrender the omega unharmed, and I allow you to walk away with generous compensation. Or resist, and suffer consequences beyond your imagination."

"Here's a third option," Sienna says, voice like steel. "You leave now, and we don't put you in the ground."

The buyer laughs, genuine amusement lighting his cold eyes. "Spirited. Exactly as promised. You'll fetch triple your already considerable price."

His hand lifts in signal, and the guards advance.

I fire twice before diving behind a boulder. *I don't kill anymore* dies somewhere between the first pull and the second. Sienna vanishes into terrain—fast, silent, using every fold of rock. The buyer's composure cracks.

"Take her alive! Kill him!"

What follows is ugly and quick. Three guards drop to my fire before the buyer's pistol catches my flank—heat punching through my side, the breath gone out of me. I stagger. The guard closest to me draws a knife and charges.

Sienna materializes behind him, branch swinging hard. He crumples. She's already shouting—"Left side!"—and I pivot, fire, drop the last guard.

The buyer stands alone among his fallen men. He raises his weapon.

We fire together. His goes wide. Mine doesn't.

The silence afterward is absolute. The buyer lies motionless, his elegant clothes stained crimson, eyes open, emptied. His remaining guard has fled, disappearing into the forest at the death of his employer.

My hands won't stop shaking. I stare at them—knuckles split, powder-burned, the same hands that wrapped her ankle with a medic's care. *I don't kill anymore* echoes back at me, hollow and already rewritten. The morning air tastes of cordite and copper and something underneath that might be relief, if relief is supposed to make your knees buckle.

"Callan." Sienna is at my side, hands pressing against the wound in my side. "How bad?"

"Through and through," I manage, though the pain makes speech difficult. "Missed anything vital. I think."

She tears strips from her shirt, binding the wound with quick hands. The adrenaline hasn't faded yet, and my body can't tell the difference—her fingers pressing against my bare skin send the same electric surge as combat, every nerve still firing, converting violence into a desperate awareness of her proximity that I have no business feeling with a bullet hole in my side. Her face is splattered with blood—not hers—but her hands are steady, her focus absolute.

"We need to move," she says. "More will come."

"Wait." I gesture toward the buyer's body. "Check his pockets. Anything with data."

She hesitates, then nods, crossing to the corpse with visible revulsion. She searches quickly, retrieving a phone, a small tablet, and a USB drive in a protective case.

"Got it."

She helps me stand, supporting my weight as we move away from the carnage, heading north toward the border. Each step sends fresh pain through my wounded side, but I force myself forward. We've come too far to falter now.

Half a mile later, safely concealed in dense forest, Sienna helps me sit against a tree trunk and checks my wound again. The bleeding has slowed, but infection is a growing risk.

"We need to get you to medical help," she says.

"Check the devices first," I urge. "Might be time-sensitive."

The tablet's screen is still lit—the buyer had been reviewing files during the standoff, and the display hasn't timed out. Sienna sees it the same instant I do and moves fast, swiping through before the lock screen catches up. Most folders are encrypted, but the one he'd been reading sits open—labeled "Northern Problem." Maps, routes, safe houses. Financial records showing millions spent hunting what the buyer called "the underground pipeline."

"It's real," she whispers. "All of it."

She turns the screen toward me. The header document maps a network beyond traditional pack law—communities where omegas are citizens, not property. Not rumor. Not wishful thinking. Proof.

One surveillance photo catches my eye before she swipes past—grainy, taken from a ridge at distance. A communal garden behind a stone wall, an omega woman hanging laundry while a child stacks kindling nearby. Smoke from a cookhouse chimney. Ordinary life, unremarkable to anyone who hasn't spent years watching people survive instead of live.

"We need to get this to Rawlins," I say.

She tucks the devices into her pack. "First, we get you patched up. I didn't fight this hard to watch you bleed out in the woods."

She helps me stand, and we move slowly northward. Toward the border. Toward something neither of us fully understands yet but both now believe in.

12

—•—

SIENNA

The outpost sits at the edge of nowhere, a weathered cabin perched on the border between what was and what might be. Three days since the buyer's death. Three days on foot, sleeping in shifts, watching for pursuit that never materialized. Callan's wound is healing clean—no infection, no complications beyond the expected pain and weakness. We're safe for now, though "safe" still feels like a foreign language. My body hasn't caught up to the quiet yet. A jay screams outside and my hand shoots to the knife on the nightstand before I register the sound—just a bird, just morning. My pulse takes a full thirty seconds to settle.

Sunlight stripes the wooden floor in gold. Callan sleeps on the narrow bed, breathing deep and even, one hand loose on the mattress where it drifted from mine in the night. I watch the slow rise and fall of his chest until something behind my ribs finally lets go.

I move to the small stove. Strike a match. Measure coffee grounds into a dented percolator. The ordinary sounds—water hissing, metal clicking against metal—fill the cabin like music I'd forgotten the tune of.

"You're thinking too loud again," Callan murmurs from the bed, voice rough with sleep.

I glance over my shoulder. "Thought you were finally getting some rest."

"Hard to rest when you're pacing mentally loud enough to wake the dead." He sits up, wincing as the movement pulls at his healing side. The bandage needs changing. I know the routine now—cleaning the wound, applying the antibiotic ointment Rawlins' people provided, wrapping fresh gauze with just the right tension.

"Let me check that," I say, bringing him coffee first, then gathering the medical supplies.

He accepts the mug with a nod of thanks, then sets it aside and lifts his shirt without being asked. The intimacy of this routine still catches me off guard sometimes—the trust in his eyes as he allows me to tend his wound, how naturally we move around each other now. Each time I change his bandage, my hands linger a little longer than strictly necessary—tracing the edge of gauze, smoothing tape against warm skin, my fingertips memorizing the topography of him as though healing requires this much touch. It doesn't. I do it anyway.

"Healing well," I observe, cleaning the puckered flesh where the bullet tore through. "Another week and we can probably switch to lighter dressing."

"Week?" He raises an eyebrow. "We staying that long?"

I secure the new bandage, considering my answer. "Rawlins says we're clear for now. The buyer's organization is in chaos with him gone. The data we recovered has disrupted three major trafficking networks already." I pause, choosing the next words carefully. "But chaos doesn't last. Organizations like that promote from within, and whoever takes his seat will want to prove themselves. The farther north we are before that happens, the better."

"That's not what I asked."

I meet his eyes, recognizing the real question beneath. Not about danger or safety or tactical considerations. About us. About what comes next.

"I don't know," I admit. "I've spent so long running from things, I'm not sure I remember how to run toward something instead."

He reaches for my hand, fingers intertwining with mine. "What do you want, Sienna? Not what's practical or safe. What do you want?"

The question hangs between us, deceptively simple. What do I want? After years of survival where want was an unaffordable luxury?

"I want…" I pause, searching for words. "I want what the woman in the transport van told me about. Places where omegas choose. Where safety isn't something granted temporarily but something lived every day."

His thumb traces circles on my palm. "The northern territories. What the riders built."

"Yes." The admission feels weighty, significant. "I want to see if it's real. If it's possible."

"According to the buyer's files, it is. A network spanning three states, moving omegas beyond traditional jurisdiction, establishing communities with different laws."

"Different laws," I repeat, testing the concept. "Places where designation doesn't determine everything."

"Places where someone like you could choose your own path." His eyes hold mine, steady and certain. "You could have that."

I notice his phrasing immediately. "Someone like me. Not us."

He looks away, that old shadow crossing his features. "I have no right to assume—"

"Stop." I catch his chin, turning his face back to mine. "After everything we've been through, are you really still trying to martyr yourself? Still believing you don't deserve more than solitude and penance?"

"Old habits," he says with a rueful smile that doesn't reach his eyes.

"Bad habits," I counter. "The same ones that almost got you killed because you thought your life was an acceptable price for my freedom."

"Sienna—"

"No." My fingers tighten on his. "I didn't fight alongside you, patch your wounds, and drag your stubborn ass through miles of wilderness just to watch you walk away at the end. If I go north, you come with me. We find that together. Or I don't go at all."

Something shifts in his expression—surprise, then a cautious hope he seems almost afraid to acknowledge. "You want me with you?"

"Yes," I say simply. "Not as protector or guide or whatever self-sacrificing role you've assigned yourself. As partner. As equal. As..." I hesitate, then push forward. "As mine. If that's what you want too."

His breath catches. For a moment, he looks almost lost, as if he's never been here before. Then slowly, deliberately, he brings my hand to his lips, pressing a kiss to my palm that feels like promise.

"Yes," he says against my skin. "That's what I want."

The simple affirmation breaks something loose inside me—a tension I've carried so long I'd forgotten it wasn't a natural part of me. I move closer, sliding onto the bed beside him, careful of his injury but needing the contact, the confirmation that this is real.

His arms come around me, drawing me against the solid warmth of his chest. Unlike our previous encounters—first tentative in the hollow, then desperate in the cabin—this embrace carries no urgency, no fear of imminent separation. Just the quiet certainty of two people who have chosen each other despite every reason not to.

When his lips find mine, the kiss is unhurried. We have time now—a luxury that makes each sensation sharper, almost unbearable. His hands trace paths they've learned—the curve of my waist, the dip of my spine, the spot below my ear that makes my breath hitch—and I answer in kind, guiding, showing, pulling his shirt up and over carefully, pressing my lips to the skin beside his bandage, tasting salt and warmth.

"Careful," he murmurs, but his hands are already sliding under my shirt, thumbs brushing the underside of my breasts, and the word has nothing to do with his wound.

I pull the fabric over my head and his eyes darken, gaze traveling over me with the same focused attention he gives everything—except now there's a heat behind it that makes my skin flush. "You're staring," I whisper.

"I'm memorizing." His voice is rough. "In case this is a dream."

I lower my mouth to his chest, tracing a line of slow kisses down his sternum while his fingers thread through my hair, his breathing growing uneven. When I straddle him, careful of his healing side, his hands settle on my hips—not guiding, just holding, letting me set the pace.

I sink onto him slowly, watching his face as I take him in—the way his jaw clenches, the way his fingers tighten on my hips, the low groan he can't contain. His scent rises warm and steady, no urgency in it, just the deep, settled alpha notes that my body has learned to read as *home*.

We find a rhythm that's neither desperate nor tentative. Just honest. I roll my hips and his thumbs trace circles on my hipbones, and everything is slow, the kind of lovemaking that feels like a conversation—question and answer, give and receive. When the tension builds, it builds gently, a warmth spreading from where we're joined until my whole body feels luminous with it.

"Open your eyes," he whispers, and I do, and his gaze holds mine as we come apart together—quiet and enormous, like dawn breaking over a landscape you didn't know you'd been waiting to see.

After, we lie tangled in morning silence, my head on his chest, his fingers tracing lazy patterns along my spine. Birds call outside, unconcerned with human matters of territory and possession.

"The contacts Rawlins gave us," Callan says. "They're part of the network—the riders. They can guide us north."

Riders. The word surfaces from the transport van's darkness, from a grey-haired woman who paid for her knowledge with a cracked skull. Not desperate fantasy. A network, and it has a name.

"When?"

"Whenever you want to go."

I rest my chin on his chest. The sanctuary I feared might be myth has already begun—not in some distant territory, but here, in the quiet certainty of being seen as an equal.

"Tomorrow," I decide. "We'll leave tomorrow."

His smile reaches his eyes this time, crinkling the corners with genuine warmth. "Tomorrow it is."

Morning stretches into afternoon, afternoon into evening, evening into our last night in the border cabin. We pack what little we own, prepare for the journey ahead. From my bag I pull the small wolf carving—retrieved from beneath its rock the morning we left the first cabin. Rough-edged, unfinished. I set it on the windowsill, facing north. A marker for whoever passes through next. The maps spread on the table show routes north, into mountains that rise blue and distant against the horizon. Territory unknown to both of us.

Dawn breaks clear and cold. Callan shoulders his pack, then helps me adjust mine.

We step outside, locking the cabin behind us. The path ahead leads through pine forest toward distant peaks, the first leg of a journey whose end we can't yet see. But for the first time in memory, I'm not running from something. I'm walking toward something instead.

"Ready?" he asks, hand finding mine.

I lace my fingers through his. "Ready."

The morning sun warms our backs as we walk north. For the first time, the future feels like a place we might actually reach.

Together.

If you want more of Sienna and Callan's story, find out what happens to them next in an exclusive bonus scene and sign up for Ash Jade's newsletter: https://free.ashjadeauthor.com/alphatracker

ALSO BY ASH JADE

Read more from Ash Jade
Short, binge-worthy omegaverse romances where
instinct burns hot and love always wins.

Lost Ridge Riders Universe

Welcome to Lost Ridge.
*Where the roads are long, the walls are guarded,
and no omega is ever owned—only chosen.*

Salt and Timber Coast Universe

Welcome to the Salt & Timber Coast.
A rain-bound peninsula where protection is steady, bonds are chosen, and love means staying.

Blackwater Bears

A quiet inland pack where bear shifters offer shelter, endurance, and a home that holds.

The Starfall Ridge Quick Reads Series

Welcome to Starfall Ridge.
Where the crater sparks scents, fate strikes fast, and no one escapes the pull of a mate.

The Yule Curse Series

Four fated nights. Four cursed alphas. One winter where heat burns brighter than fire.

The Touch Her and Die Series

In a world ruled by dominance, instinct, and the pull of fate, every story begins with danger—and ends with devotion.

<u>The Sanctuary Pack Series</u>

Welcome to Sanctuary.
A hidden mountain town where omegas come to heal—and alphas learn what it means to protect.

About Ash Jade

Ash Jade writes trope-packed omegaverse romances full of heat, ruts, and fated mates — but always with heart. Her stories are fast, messy, and addictive, blending primal passion with emotional cores that make the bonds hit even harder. If you love bingeable romances where instinct tangles with feelings (and always ends in happily-ever-after), you've found your pack.

ashjadeauthor.com

www.ingramcontent.com/pod-product-compliance
Lightning Source LLC
Chambersburg PA
CBHW021129070726
47591CB00014B/2034